ROB THE MOLE
AND THE
SNEAKY GNOME

MAGIC E AND THE LONG O SOUND

By BLAKE HOENA

Illustrations by LUKE FLOWERS

Music by MARK OBLINGER

CANTATA
LEARNING

WWW.CANTATALEARNING.COM

CANTATA
LEARNING

Published by Cantata Learning
1710 Roe Crest Drive
North Mankato, MN 56003
www.cantatalearning.com

A note to educators and librarians from the publisher: Cantata Learning has provided the following data to assist in book processing and suggested use of Cantata Learning product.

Publisher's Cataloging-in-Publication Data
Prepared by Librarian Consultant: Ann-Marie Begnaud
Library of Congress Control Number: 2016938092
    Rob the Mole and the Sneaky Gnome : Magic E and the Long O Sound
    Series: Read, Sing, Learn
    By Blake Hoena
    Illustrations by Luke Flowers
    Music by Mark Oblinger
    Summary: The wizard Magic E teaches readers how the silent e changes words like cod to code, giving them a long O sound, in this outlandish story set to music.
    ISBN: 978-1-63290-791-2 (library binding/CD)
Suggested Dewey and Subject Headings:
    Dewey: E FIC
    LCSH Subject Headings: Wizards – Juvenile humor. | Wizards – Songs and music – Texts. | Wizards – Juvenile sound recordings.
    Sears Subject Headings: Magic. | Phonetics. | School songbooks. | Children's songs. | Rock music.
    BISAC Subject Headings: JUVENILE FICTION / Fantasy & Magic. | JUVENILE FICTION / Stories in Verse. | JUVENILE FICTION / Humorous stories.

Book design and art direction: Tim Palin Creative
Editorial direction: Flat Sole Studio
Music direction: Elizabeth Draper
Music written and produced by Mark Oblinger

Printed in the United States of America in North Mankato, Minnesota.
122016   0339CGS17

ACCESS THE MUSIC!
SCAN CODE WITH MOBILE APP
CANTATALEARNING.COM

TIPS TO SUPPORT LITERACY AT HOME

WHY READING AND SINGING WITH YOUR CHILD IS SO IMPORTANT

Daily reading with your child leads to increased academic achievement. Music and songs, specifically rhyming songs, are a fun and easy way to build early literacy and language development. Music skills correlate significantly with both phonological awareness and reading development. Singing helps build vocabulary and speech development. And reading and appreciating music together is a wonderful way to strengthen your relationship.

READ AND SING EVERY DAY!

TIPS FOR USING CANTATA LEARNING BOOKS AND SONGS DURING YOUR DAILY STORY TIME

1. As you sing and read, point out the different words on the page that rhyme. Suggest other words that rhyme.

2. Memorize simple rhymes such as Itsy Bitsy Spider and sing them together. This encourages comprehension skills and early literacy skills.

3. Use the questions in the back of each book to guide your singing and storytelling.

4. Read the included sheet music with your child while you listen to the song. How do the music notes correlate to the words of the song?

5. Sing along on the go and at home. Access music by scanning the QR code on each Cantata book, or by using the included CD. You can also stream or download the music for free to your computer, smartphone, or mobile device.

Devoting time to daily reading shows that you are available for your child. Together, you are building language, literacy, and listening skills.

Have fun reading and singing!

Have you heard of the Magic E? When added to the end of some words, it changes their vowel sound. For example, *cod* becomes *code* and *Rob* becomes *robe*. Sometimes Magic E is called the Silent E because it does this trick without making a sound.

Now Al-la-ke-zee! Ke-zo-ke-zoe! What can the wizard Magic E do with an *E*?

Turn the page to see! Remember to sing along!

Rob the **Mole** hoped to be a **special agent**, to break secret **codes** and face real danger.

So off he went in search of Magic E,
a wizard who could do cool trickery.

Oh, do you know what Magic E told Rob the Mole?

"Al-la-ke-zee! Ke-zo-ke-zoe-oe-oe!
With an *E*, this cod can read any code."

Oh, do you know what Magic E told Rob the Mole?

"Al-la-ke-zee! Ke-zo-ke-zoe-oe-oe!
With an *E*, Rob, you'll get a special robe."

Rob got in a red **hot rod**, and off he rode.

Rob the Mole spotted a sneaky **gnome**,
a **crook** who had stolen a sparkly stone.

14

The gnome hopped away, quickly as a toad,
but left behind a note with a top-secret code.

Oh, do you know what Magic E told Rob the Mole?

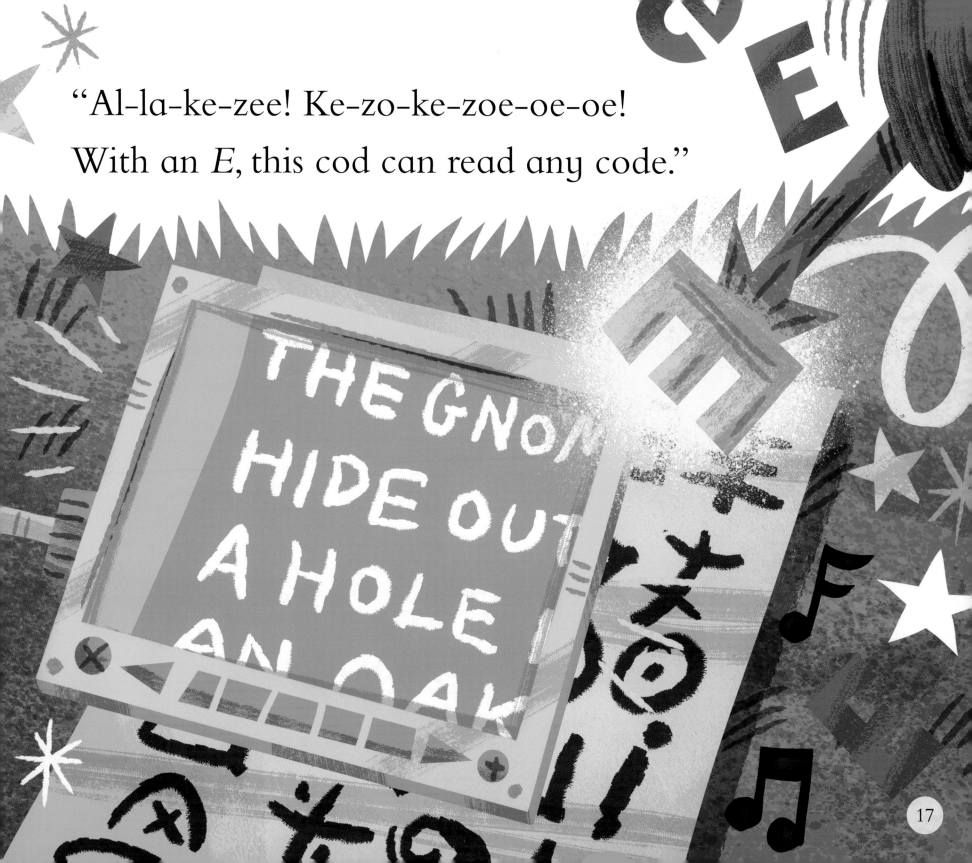

"Al-la-ke-zee! Ke-zo-ke-zoe-oe-oe!
With an *E*, this cod can read any code."

THE GNOM
HIDE OUT
A HOLE
AN OAK

The top-secret note told Rob where to go
if he wanted to catch that **pesky** gnome.

So Rob got in his hot rod, and off he rode
after that gnome who hopped away like a toad.

Oh, do you know what Magic E told Rob the Mole?

"Al-la-ke-zee! Ke-zo-ke-zoe-oe-oe!
With an *E*, Rob, you'll get a special robe.

Al-la-ke-zee! Ke-zo-ke-zoe-oe-oe!"

SONG LYRICS
Rob the Mole and the Sneaky Gnome

Rob the Mole hoped to be a special agent,
to break secret codes and face real danger.
So off he went in search of Magic E,
a wizard who could do cool trickery.

Oh, do you know what Magic E told Rob the Mole?
"Al-la-ke-zee! Ke-zo-ke-zoe-oe-oe!
With an E, this cod can read any code."

Oh, do you know what Magic E told Rob the Mole?
"Al-la-ke-zee! Ke-zo-ke-zoe-oe-oe!
With an E, Rob, you'll get a special robe."

Rob got in a red hot rod, and off he rode.
He was singing,
"Hip, hop, hope, oh, yeah!
Nit, not, note, all right!
Slip, slop, slope, yo, yo!
Rid, rod, rode, here I go!"

Rob the Mole spotted a sneaky gnome,
a crook who had stolen a sparkly stone.
The gnome hopped away, quickly as a toad,
but left behind a note with a top-secret code.

Oh, do you know what Magic E told Rob the Mole?
"Al-la-ke-zee! Ke-zo-ke-zoe-oe-oe!
With an E, this cod can read any code."

The top-secret note told Rob where to go
if he wanted to catch that pesky gnome.
So Rob got in his hot rod, and off he rode
after that gnome who hopped away like a toad.

Oh, do you know what Magic E told Rob the Mole?
"Al-la-ke-zee! Ke-zo-ke-zoe-oe-oe!
With an E, Rob, you'll get a special robe.
Al-la-ke-zee! Ke-zo-ke-zoe-oe-oe!"

Rob the Mole and the Sneaky Gnome

Rock
Mark Oblinger

Chorus
Oh, do you know what Magic E told Rob the Mole?
"Al-la-ke-zee! Ke-zo-ke-zoe-oe-oe!
With an E, Rob, you'll get a special robe."

Verse 2
Rob the Mole spotted a sneaky gnome,
a crook who had stolen a sparkly stone.
The gnome hopped away, quickly as a toad,
but left behind a note with a top-secret code.

Chorus
Oh, do you know what Magic E told Rob the Mole?
"Al-la-ke-zee! Ke-zo-ke-zoe-oe-oe!
With an E, this cod can read any code."

Verse 3
The top-secret note told Rob where to go
if he wanted to catch that pesky gnome.
So Rob got in his hot rod, and off he rode
after that gnome who hopped away like a toad.

Chorus
Oh, do you know what Magic E told Rob the Mole?
"Al-la-ke-zee! Ke-zo-ke-zoe-oe-oe!
With an E, Rob, you'll get a special robe.

GLOSSARY

codes—systems of symbols that stand for letters

crook—a criminal

gnome—in fairy tales, a little old man who has a beard and guards treasures underground

hot rod—a fast car

mole—a furry animal that lives underground

pesky—annoying

special agent—a detective

GUIDED READING ACTIVITIES

1. Go for a walk outside. How many things can you see that end with Magic E? Do you see a kite, a rope, a cane, or a rose? Can you come up with five words on your own?

2. In this book, the wizard Magic E is an owl. What if the wizard were a different animal? Draw a picture of the wizard as your favorite animal.

3. Listen to the song again. Every time you hear a word that uses Magic E, make a tally mark. How many marks did you make?

TO LEARN MORE

Bolger, Kevin. *Lazy Bear, Crazy Bear: Loony Long Vowels*. New York: HarperCollins, 2015.

Gregory, Jillian. *Breaking Secret Codes*. North Mankato, MN: Capstone, 2011.

Pulver, Robin. *Happy Endings: A Story about Suffixes*. New York: Holiday House, 2011.

Rake, Jody S. *Meerkats, Moles, and Voles: Animals of the Underground*. North Mankato, MN: Capstone, 2016.